ZONDERkidz **I Can Read!**™

BEGINNING 1 READING

The Case of the Couch Potato Caper

D0003062

story by Karen Poth

My name is Detective Larry.

This is my partner, Bob.

We solve mysteries.
Sometimes our jobs
are very messy.
Here is one of our stories.

It was the middle of the afternoon.

We were cleaning our desks.

Police Chief Scooter came in.

Laura Carrot had been taken prisoner!

We needed to hurry.

We went to the Carrot home.

It looked bad!

"It's the Couch Potatoes,"
Scooter said.
"The laziest potatoes
in town."

"Since they came, Laura has done nothing but watch TV!" Scooter said.

"How did they get in?" I asked.

"Laura was getting lazy," Scooter said.

"That's when they came."

I got out my bullhorn.

"COME OUT, COME OUT,
WHEREVER YOU ARE!" I said.

My bullhorn was really loud!

"WHAT SHOULD I SAY NEXT?"

I asked Bob through the bullhorn.

It was too loud.

Bob said I was rude.

"PLEASE, COME OUT!" I said.

The potatoes didn't answer.

15

We saw Laura's mother.

"How did this happen?"

Bob asked.

"I don't know," she said.

"Laura won't do her chores.

Her room is a mess.

She even lost her homework."

Just then more police came.

They had remote controls.

They aimed them at the TV

in the house.

They hit their "off" buttons.

Bull's-eye!

Laura's TV turned off.

Bob and I snuck in the back door.

Laura's room was a mess!
There were toys and clothes
all over the floor.
The Couch Potatoes
turned the TV back on.
The police turned it off.
On, off, on, off, on, off …

"Hold it right there," I said.
A potato pulled out
a big snack-shooter.
"We are not giving up," he said.

"Laura," Bob said.

"You need to stop being so lazy.

God wants us to work hard."

"But I like watching TV
all day," Laura said.
"It's fun!"
"Look at this room," Bob said.
"It's a mess."

Then I got an idea.

I started cleaning up.

Bob helped.

We found lots of
lost things.

We found Laura's dolls.

We found her bears

and her unicycle.

We even found her
lost homework paper.
"Thank you," Laura said.
"Now I don't have to
do my homework again!

I can't believe I
lost all these things.
Being lazy isn't so great
after all," she said.

The Couch Potatoes packed
their snacks and left.
Laura and her mom
thanked us for our hard work.
Another happy ending!

3 1333 04166 1263